DILYS PRICE

NORMAN
PRICE

BELLA
LASAGNE

JAMES

MEET ALL THESE FRIENDS IN BUZZ BOOKS:

Thomas the Tank Engine
Fireman Sam
Looney Tunes
Tiny Toon Adventures
Bugs Bunny
Toucan 'Tecs
Flintstones
Jetsons
Joshua Jones

First published by Buzz Books,
an imprint of Reed Consumer Books Ltd
Michelin House, 81 Fulham Road, London SW3 6RB

LONDON MELBOURNE AUCKLAND

ISBN 1 85591 254 6

Printed and bound in the UK by BPCC Hazell Books Ltd

FLOUR POWER

Story by Rob Lee
Illustrations by The County Studio

The Newtown Fire Brigade needed extra help one morning, so Fireman Sam and Firefighter Elvis Cridlington arrived from Pontypandy. They were also collecting a supply of new fire hoses from Newtown Fire Station.

Firefighter Penny Morris showed them how to use the new hoses.

"These high-powered hoses are very effective in large fires, but they need to be handled carefully," she said.

She aimed the nozzle at a tree on the edge of the forecourt and turned on the hose. A powerful stream of water drenched the tree in seconds.

"Daro, look at that!" Sam exclaimed. "This hose could douse the whole of Pontypandy High Street in no time!"

"Let me try," said Elvis enthusiastically.
"I'm a dab hand with hoses."

But the water surged through the hose
so quickly that Elvis lost his grip and the
nozzle whirled into the air, showering
water all over him.

"Help!" spluttered Elvis. "I'm getting wet!"
Penny turned off the water supply.

"A dab hand, eh?" chuckled Fireman Sam.

"I just need some practice," Elvis replied.

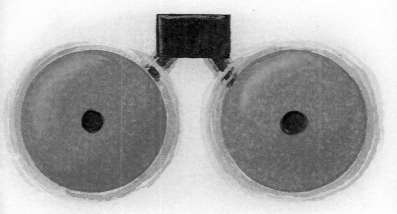

Just then the alarm sounded.

"You'll have to practise on the job, I'm
afraid," said Penny. She checked the message
on the telex. "There's a fire at Newtown
Bakery!" she cried. "Let's go!"

Penny jumped into Venus, while Fireman Sam and Elvis jumped into Jupiter. With lights flashing and sirens blaring, the fire engines raced to the bakery.

"We'll need our most powerful equipment to fight this blaze," said Penny through her breathing apparatus. She unloaded one of the high-powered hoses. "Elvis, you cordon off the road. Sam and I will tackle the fire."

Meanwhile, Sarah, James and Norman were going to Newtown in Trevor's bus.

"You're going to meet Sam at Newtown Fire Station, are you?" said Trevor.

"Yes, Uncle Sam's taking us to the cinema this afternoon," Sarah said excitedly.

"We're going to see a horror film," added Norman. "It's all about ghosts. I think ghosts are brill, don't you?"

Before Trevor had a chance to answer, he spotted a roadblock up ahead. "Daro, I wonder what the problem is," he groaned. "I'm afraid you'll have to walk the rest of the way from here, children. And be sure you stay well away from the trouble."

At the bakery, Fireman Sam and Penny had finally got the fire under control.

"These high-powered hoses are just the ticket," said Sam.

"We won't need this breathing apparatus now," said Penny as she took off her mask and oxygen tank. "I'll hose down the rest of the building so the fire doesn't spread."

As Sam was extinguishing the remaining embers, Elvis arrived.

"Mission accomplished," called Elvis. "Everyone's safe."

"Good work," said Sam. "The fire is nearly out now, so you can help Firefighter Morris douse the rest of the building."

"Righto, Fireman Sam," replied Elvis.

Elvis found Penny in the storeroom.

"Why doesn't my fresh baked bread taste as good as Newtown Bakery's?" he wondered as he sprayed the storeroom with water.

"Make sure you've got a good grip on the hose this time," Penny advised.

"Don't worry," replied Elvis confidently.

But a moment later, a barrel labelled 'Secret Ingredient' caught his eye. "Hmm, I wonder what that could be—"

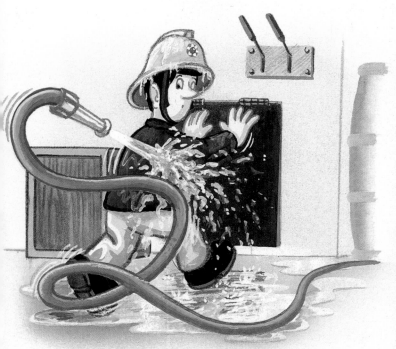

Elvis didn't have time to find out, as the hose suddenly flew out of his hands, soaking him for the second time that day. Quickly, Elvis dashed for cover through a little door in the wall of the storeroom.

17

"Elvis, that's the flour chute!" warned Penny.

But it was too late. Elvis was already speeding down the chute.

"Now I know what the secret ingredient is," he thought. "Me!"

18

Suddenly, Elvis landed in a huge
mountain of flour.

"Are you all right, Elvis?" called Penny
from above.

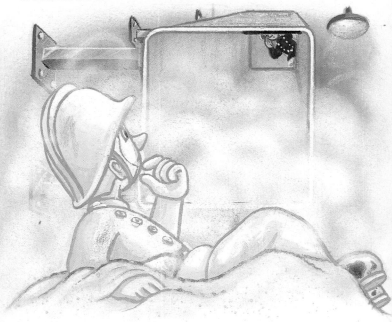

"I think so," answered Elvis. He looked
down at himself. He was covered from head
to toe with flour!

"Lucky for you it was a soft landing,"
chuckled Penny.

Outside, the children were walking around the cordoned off area towards Newtown.

"There's been a fire at the bakery," observed Norman. "I'll bet Fireman Sam is there. Let's go and see."

"We're not supposed to go near the fire,
Norman. That's what the barriers are for,"
James reminded him.

"But it looks like the fire's been put out
already," replied Norman. "Come on."

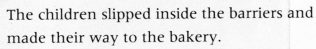

The children slipped inside the barriers and made their way to the bakery.

"I can't wait to see the horror film this afternoon. I hope the ghosts are really scary," said Norman.

At that very moment, Elvis climbed out
of the bakery basement and nearly bumped
into the children. Norman stared at Elvis
in disbelief.

"It's a gh-ghost!" he cried.

He ran away as fast as he could, followed
closely by James and Sarah.

The children raced towards Sam and Penny,
who were replacing the hoses in Venus.

"Great fires of London!" said Fireman Sam.
"What are you children doing here? Didn't
you see the barriers?"

"You look as if you've seen a ghost,"
added Penny.

"We have!" cried Norman. "Look!"

They turned to look at Elvis as he sprinted towards them, still covered with flour from head to toe. Sam and Penny laughed.

"Oh yes, the famous ghost of Newtown Bakery," chuckled Fireman Sam, "otherwise known as Firefighter Elvis Cridlington."

"Elvis?!" said Sarah.

"Y-you mean you're not a ghost?" stammered Norman.

"Sorry to disappoint you, Norman," laughed Elvis. He patted his uniform and a puff of white dust floated into the air. "I'm just covered in baking flour, that's all."

"Let's go back to the station and get cleaned up," said Penny. She turned to the children. "Next time you see safety barriers, make sure to go around them," she said.

"We won't do it again," said James.

"Come on, you children can ride to Newtown in the fire engines," said Sam.

"Brill!" replied all three children together.

It was too late to go to the cinema, so Sam took the children to Bella's café instead.

"Perhaps we can go to see the film tomorrow," he suggested.

"No thanks, Uncle Sam," replied Sarah. "We've had enough of ghosts for a while."

"Then how about something that will really send a shiver down your spine?" said Sam in a spooky voice.

"Wh-what's that?" gulped Norman.

"Strawberry ice-creams all round," laughed Fireman Sam.

FIREMAN SAM

STATION OFFICER
STEELE

TREVOR EVANS

ELVIS
CRIDLINGTON

PENNY MORRIS